OCTOPUS'S GARDEN

I'd like to dedicate this book
to octopuses everywhere.
Peace & Love,
Ringo

For Ruth, Johnny and Anna
with all my love,
Ben

SIMON AND SCHUSTER

First published in Great Britain in 2013 by Simon and Schuster UK Ltd
1st Floor, 222 Gray's Inn Road, London WC1X 8HB
A CBS COMPANY

This paperback edition first published 2015

A CIP catalogue record for this book is available from
the British Library upon request

ISBN: 978-1-4711-2007-7 (HB+AUDIO CD)
ISBN: 978-1-4711-2022-0 (PB)
ISBN: 978-1-4711-2021-3 (eBook)
Printed in China
1 3 5 7 9 10 8 6 4 2

OCTOPUS'S GARDEN

RINGO STARR
Illustrated by Ben Cort

SIMON AND SCHUSTER
London New York Sydney Toronto New Delhi

I'd like to be under the sea
In an octopus's garden in the shade.

He'd let us in, knows where we've been
In his octopus's garden in the shade.

I'd ask my friends to come and see
An octopus's garden with me.

I'd like to be under the sea
In an octopus's garden in the shade.

We would be warm below the storm

In our little hideaway beneath the waves.

Resting our head on the seabed
In an octopus's garden near a cave.

We would sing and dance around
Because we know we can't be found.

I'd like to be under the sea
In an octopus's garden in the shade.

We would shout and swim about
The coral that lies beneath the waves
(Lies beneath the ocean waves).

Oh what joy for every girl and boy
Knowing they're happy and they're safe
(Happy and they're safe).

We would be so happy you and me
No one there to tell us what to do.

I'd like to be under the sea
In an octopus's garden with **YOU**.

Scan the code for a free audio reading
of this book **by Ringo Starr** and
a very special version of the song.

It's a magical underwater adventure!